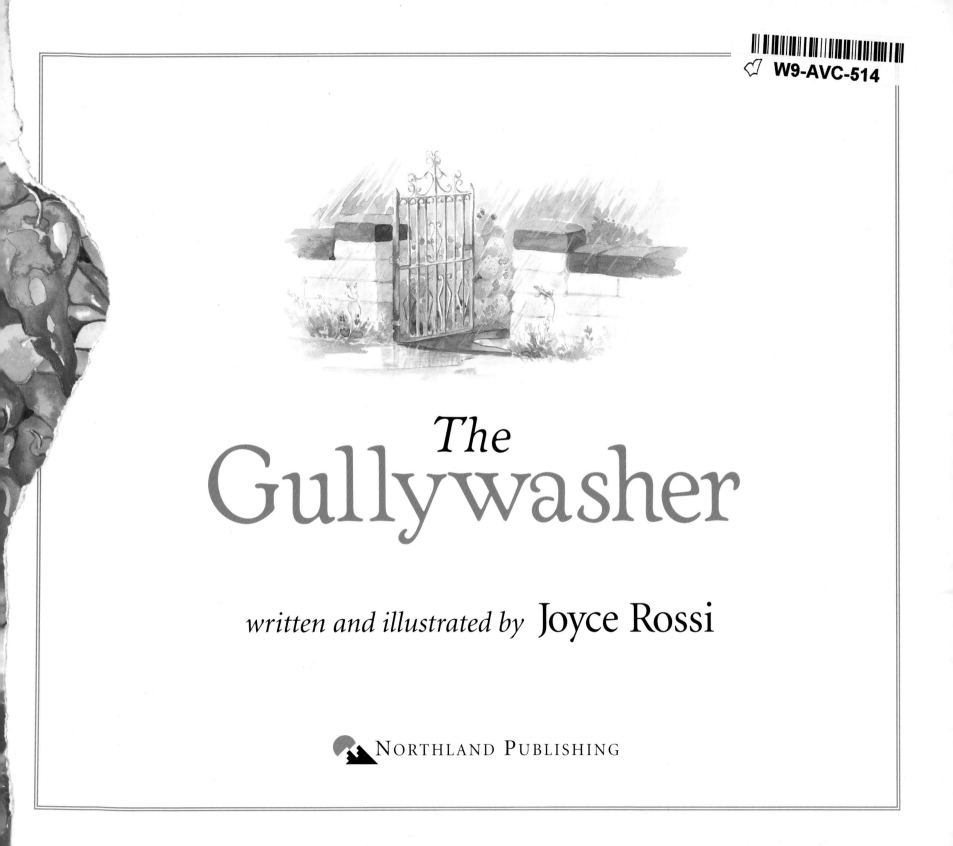

The
Gullywasher

written and illustrated by Joyce Rossi

NORTHLAND PUBLISHING

To my parents, Hazel and Harold Muller;

and to the cowboy poet Jack Walther, who inspired this story.

Special thanks to Dave and Diane Beling and to Jane Smith of Safford, Arizona;
to Leticia Le Garda and her beautiful family of Fort Thomas, Arizona; to Leticia's teacher
Pati Hinton; and to Jim and Natalie Brock, and Dorothy Miller of Verdi, Nevada.

The paintings were done in watercolor on
300 lb. Fabriano Artistico hot pressed paper
The text type was set in Minion
The display type was set in Artcraft
Designed by Rudy J. Ramos
Edited by Katy Spining

Manufactured in Hong Kong by
South Sea International Press Ltd.

FIRST IMPRESSION
ISBN 0-87358-607-7

Library of Congress Catalog Card Number 95-116544
Library of Congress Cataloging-in-Publication Data
Rossi, Joyce.
The gullywasher / written and illustrated by Joyce Rossi. — 1st ed.
p.   cm.
Summary: Leticia's grandfather, who was a vaquero as a young man,
provides fanciful explanations for how he got his wrinkles,
white hair, round belly, and stooped frame.
ISBN 0-87358-607-7
1. Grandfathers—Fiction. [1. Cowboys—Fiction.
2. Storms—Fiction. 3. Tall Tales.] I. Title.
PZ7.R7215Gu 1995
[E]—dc20   95-116544

0540/7.5M/9-95

A Note from the Author

When the grandfather in this story was a young man, and for many years before, cattle roamed the western rangeland freely. Since there were few or no fences, cattle owners hired horsemen to tend their stock. Mexican horsemen, called *vaqueros*, were the first cowboys (or buckaroos).

Life on the range was harsh. Among the greatest dangers were the gullywashers, or thundershowers, that struck during the spring and summer. These violent storms often caused flash floods and stampedes. But of all the cowboy's hardships, the greatest was loneliness.

There were times, perhaps during a roundup, when cowboys joined their fellow workers around a campfire to sing songs or tell stories. Some of their favorite tales were about men, like themselves, who faced difficult tasks. But in these tall tales, the hero always won. With each telling, the stories grew more outrageous. The storyteller would keep a straight face to convince the listener that the unbelievable story was true. This made the listener laugh even more.

Tall tales were sometimes called whoppers, windies, gallyfloppers, or yarns. They demonstrate cowboys' love of sharing laughter among friends, much as Leticia and her grandfather share *The Gullywasher*.

Leticia and her grandfather watched the summer rain clouds drift across the southwestern sky.

"Now *that* was a gullywasher," said Leticia's grandfather. "We'd better wait a minute before we take our walk. It could start up again."

Leticia climbed onto the arm of the old stuffed chair.

"Look at me, Abuelito. Giddyap!" she shouted.

"Hey, little *vaquera*," said her grandfather as he sank into the cushion beside her. "You got room in your saddlebag for an old-timer like me?"

"*Sí*," answered Leticia, bouncing up and down.

"Where are you off to so fast?" asked Abuelito.

"I'm going to round up cattle and take them back to the *rancho,* just like you used to do."

Leticia twirled an imaginary lasso above her head and gave it a toss.

"Tell me about when you were a *vaquero,*" she said.

"That was a long time ago. I think I forgot," teased Abuelito.

"No, you haven't. You remember. Please," begged Leticia.

"Ohhhh, yes," began Abuelito slowly. "I remember a spring day, many years ago, when the biggest gullywasher ever came my way. I was searching for stray cattle just south of here. The sky turned dark as night. Dust devils came whipping off the mesas, blowing my sombrero high up into the sky. The rain began.

And it wouldn't stop.

"I looked for shelter, but there wasn't any. I had to let the rain wash over me.

"After the storm was finally over, I saw how the water had wrinkled my hands. When I looked at my reflection in a water hole, I could see that the rain had wrinkled my face, too. And that's the way I've looked ever since."

Leticia laughed. She reached over and ruffled her grandfather's fluffy white hair.

"And how did you get this?" she asked.

"I climbed back on my horse and rode until I was too tired to go on. I stopped to take a siesta in the shade of a palo verde.

"While I slept, a hummingbird began to take strands of my hair to make her nest. That *pajarita* was so gentle and quiet, I never woke. One by one she plucked the dark-colored hairs, but she left all the white ones for me."

Leticia giggled and patted her grandfather's round belly. "Now, tell me how you got this."

"I was very hungry when I woke up. But I had no food, so I rode on until I came to a village. There, an old woman was sitting in front of her house, grinding corn on her *metate*. I asked her if she could spare a handful, and she gave me some of the hard kernels.

"I swallowed them whole, but I was still hungry. So I gobbled some chile peppers hanging on the wall nearby. The old woman jumped up and began to wave. 'No, *vaquero!*' she shouted. But it was too late. The chiles were as hot as fire. They made the corn pop, pop, pop, and my stomach grew, grew, grew."

"Pop, pop, pop," said Leticia, jumping off the chair and hopping around the porch. "Look, the clouds are going away. Let's go for our walk now. I'll pull you up."

The smell of the damp desert was strong and sweet. Leticia jumped over the puddles and skipped circles around Abuelito as he moved slowly down the road.

"Abuelito, why are you so bent over?" asked Leticia.

"Did that also happen on the day of the big gullywasher?"

"As a matter of fact, it did," said her grandfather.

"I climbed onto my horse to begin the long journey
home. But the horse was tired and wouldn't budge. I
tried to push him and I tried to pull him, but he stood
solid as a mountain."

"What did you do?" asked Leticia.

"Well," said Abuelito, "I swung that *caballo* over my shoulders and carried him all the way home on my back."

They stopped to rest at the mission. Leticia became very quiet.

"What's the matter?" said Abuelito. "It's not like you to be so still."

"Does it make you sad to be bent over?" Leticia asked.

Abuelito thought for a minute.

"No, little *vaquera,*" he said as they began their walk home. "It makes me closer to you." And he stooped, just a little, to kiss her forehead.

Glossary

Here are some Spanish words and their pronunciations to help you enjoy this story. By the way, Leticia's name is pronounced (lay-TEE-sha).

Abuelito (ah-bway-LEE-to). Dearest grandfather.

caballo (kah-BAH-yo). Horse.

mesa (MAY-sa). A plateau or flat area of land. Mesa also means table in the Spanish language.

metate (meh-TAH-tay). A flat stone upon which corn and other grain may be ground into flour.

pajarita (pah-hah-REE-ta). Little bird (female).

palo verde (PAH-lo VER-day). The palo verde is Arizona's state tree. *Palo* is the Spanish word for stick and *verde* is the Spanish word for green.

rancho (RAN-cho). Ranch.

sí (SEE). Yes.

siesta (see-ES-ta). An afternoon nap.

vaquera (vah-KAY-ra). Cowgirl.

vaquero (vah-KAY-ro). Cowboy.

JOYCE ROSSI was inspired to write her first children's picture book by her childhood heroes, Paul Bunyan, Davy Crockett, and Johnny Appleseed. Believing nothing was impossible, these characters always responded to their challenges in imaginative and humorous ways.

Although *The Gullywasher* is the first book she has written, Joyce previously illustrated *Winker, Buttercup and Blue,* by Arlene Williams (Waking Light Press).

Joyce lives in Verdi, Nevada, with her husband, Lou. She is a graduate of the University of Nevada, Reno, with a degree in elementary education. She currently teaches art to children and adults in her home. Besides traveling, she and her husband enjoy hiking in the beautiful Sierra Nevada Mountains.